DOG LOVES COUNTING

LOUISE YATES

Jonathan Cape
London

For Owen

Some other books by Louise Yates
A Small Surprise
Dog Loves Books
Dog Loves Drawing
Frank & Teddy Make Friends

DOG LOVES COUNTING
A JONATHAN CAPE BOOK 978 0 857 55015 6

Published in Great Britain by Jonathan Cape,
an imprint of Random House Children's Books
A Random House Group Company

This edition published 2013

1 3 5 7 9 10 8 6 4 2

Copyright © Louise Yates, 2013

The right of Louise Yates to be identified as the author and illustrator of this work has been asserted
in accordance with the Copyright, Designs and Patents Act 1988.

All rights reserved.

RANDOM HOUSE CHILDREN'S BOOKS
61–63 Uxbridge Road, London W5 5SA

www.**kids**at**randomhouse**.co.uk
www.**randomhouse**.co.uk

Addresses for companies within The Random House Group Limited can be found at: www.randomhouse.co.uk/offices.htm

THE RANDOM HOUSE GROUP Limited Reg. No. 954009

A CIP catalogue record for this book is available from the British Library.

Printed in China

Dog loved books. He loved reading
them late into the night and didn't like
to leave them for long.

He knew he must
sleep, but Dog
just couldn't drift
off. He tried
counting sheep,
but they weren't
helping at all.

"Perhaps there are other creatures

Dog reached for a book and began.

The first thing Dog found was an egg.

"One," he counted, and the egg began to hatch.

Inside was a baby dodo.
"Hello, little one," said Dog.
He looked around, but
the dodo was
all alone.

Nº 2
Dog

Nº 1
The Dodo

"I'll look after you," said Dog. "Together
we are two. Number One, follow me –
we must find Number Three."

They looked on through the book for
the next creature they could count.
"Number Three?" Dog called out.

"Are you speaking to
me?" said a sloth
after a long silence.
He waved very, very slowly.

1 2 3

Nº3
The
Three-Toed
Sloth

Dog counted his claws.

The three-toed sloth wanted to help them find more numbers. He took his time, but together they continued on, keeping count all the way.

1... 2...3...

"Four!" cried a camel. "One, two, three, four!"
He counted out on his legs.
"We are counting," explained Dog,
"so that I can fall asleep."

The camel hoped he could help. "In the desert
where I come from, there are many more things
we can count. Follow me!"

Nº4
The Camel

1

2   3   4

"The next number is five," said the camel. "There is a lizard, I think, called a five-lined skink."

They found him under a log.

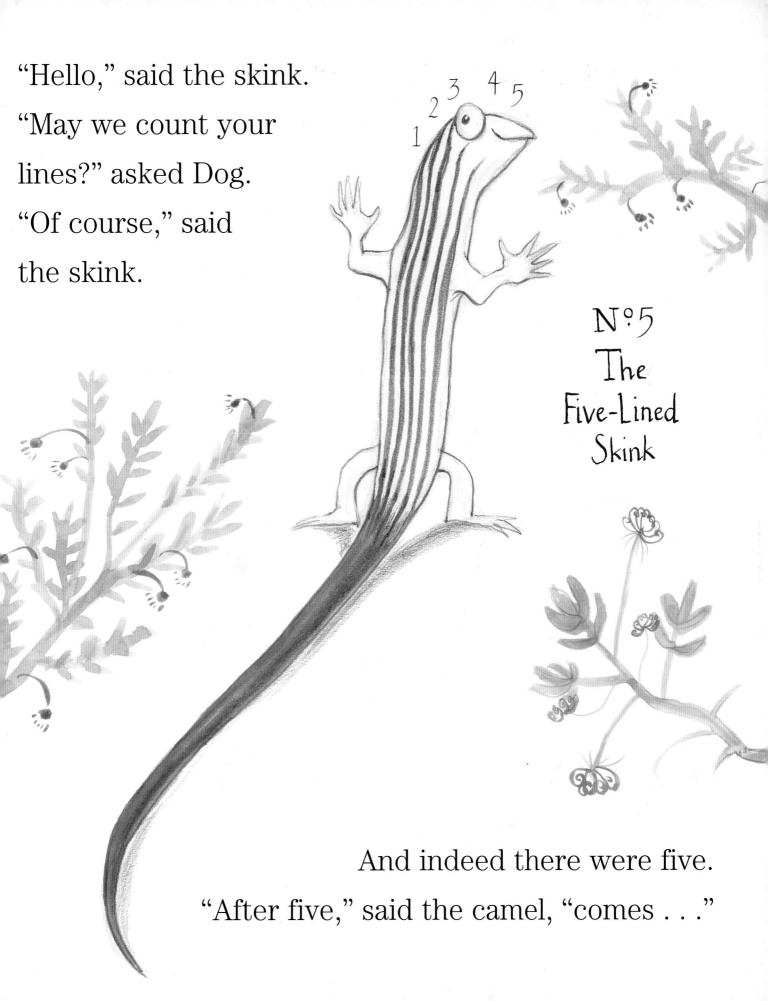

"Hello," said the skink.
"May we count your
lines?" asked Dog.
"Of course," said
the skink.

N° 5
The
Five-Lined
Skink

And indeed there were five.
"After five," said the camel, "comes . . ."

"Six!" said the skink
with his mouth full.

And as he untangled the fly, they quickly saw why.

1 2 3 4 5 6

N°6
The Fly

"Coooo-eeee!" called a . . .

. . . raccoon, waving her tail.

She had seven black stripes.

Nº7
The Raccoon

1 2

3

4

5   6   7

"We're on our way to the desert," said Dog.

"Can I come too?" called a spider. "Or am I too late?"

1
2
3
4
5
6
7
8

N°8
The Spider

"Just in time," replied Dog, and they counted to eight.

Number Nine was harder to find –

he was dozing in his burrow.

"Who's in there?" called Dog.

"A nine-banded armadillo," said a voice.

N°9
The Nine-Banded
Armadillo

123456789

And when the creature came out, they saw it was true.

He joined them too.

"Nearly there," said the camel.

"What number's next?" asked the armadillo.

"Ten!" called a crab, and he scuttled about waving each leg in turn.

Nº10
The Crab

1

10

2

3

4

5

6

7

8

9

Dog was enjoying himself!
He couldn't wait to know
more numbers.

But when at last they did reach the desert, Dog was disappointed. There was nothing to count as far as he could see.

"Don't worry," said the camel. "There are as many numbers here as there are grains of sand beneath our feet."

"Let's all count together," said Dog cheerfully.
"Number One . . ." he began.

But Number One was nowhere to be seen!

"We've lost One!"
cried Dog.
"We must find him!"

They were all
very worried.

So they split up and set off, searching in different directions.

There were ten, 10

then nine, 9

then eight, 8

then seven, 7

then six, 6

then five,
5

then four,
4

then three,
3

then two,
2

and then . . .

. . . there was # One.

He was looking up at the stars.
They all joined him, counting up and up,
higher and higher and higher.

Dog loves counting!

"I could do this for ever," he said
happily. The others agreed.

When Dog woke up the next morning and looked
at his books, he knew that friends and adventures
were never far away – that was something
he could count on.